COVER ~~ BY
SCOTTIE

HEY
GRANDMA!

WRITTEN BY:

SCOTTIE B. CALDWELL AND DEAN CHRISTOPHER CALDWELL

ISBN: 978-1957547749

Published in 2023 by Scribe Marketer
This book is based on the actual conversations between a grandmother and grandson.

Media.diva.pro@gmail.com

Dedication

First, I want to thank my amazing grandson and co-author Dean Caldwell. Special thanks to Alan Knox for being the "superman" and world's best grandpa in Dean's life.

This book is also a tribute to my children, Christian and Julius. Your love and encouragement means the world to me. Lastly, this book is dedicated to the memory of my parents, Dr. Virgil J. Caldwell and Ruby W. Caldwell. My first teachers and my heroes.

Written by

Scottie B. Caldwell and Dean Christopher Caldwell

This book is about the relationship between a grandma and her grandson. Dean is a 5 year old with a burning curiosity to life's essential questions. His grandma may not have all the correct answers, but she addresses his questions so he can understand to the best of his ability.

Curiosity is one of the most important skills to learn.

Dean's Tips:
- Don't ever be afraid to ASK questions.
- If something doesn't make sense, ASK.
- Never stop ASKING questions.

Grandma's Tips:
- Give your grandchildren the chance to stretch their creative mind. They in turn will be able to later solve their own problems more easily. Be your child's biggest cheerleader while they are in their exploration phase.

- Help your child feel competent and confident. Never speak baby-talk. You want them to show progression in their vocabulary, not regression. Their brains are like a sponge, they absorb everything.

- Last, always reassure them that they are forever loved.

Love at first sight.

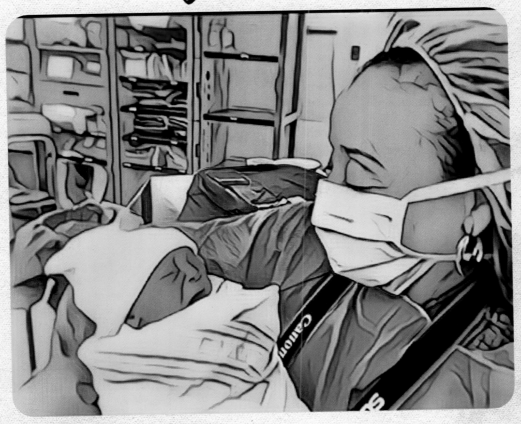

DEAN SCREAMS, "HEY GRANDMA! WHY ARE WE HERE TO SEE MY GREAT-GRANDPARENTS WHEN YOU SAID THEY WERE IN HEAVEN?"

GRANDMA SAYS, "I USUALLY BRING YOU HERE ON SPECIAL OCCASIONS LIKE THEIR BIRTHDAY. IF YOU LOOK CLOSELY, THE TOMBSTONES HAVE THEIR NAMES ON THEM. EVEN THOUGH THEIR BODIES ARE HERE, THEIR SOULS ARE IN HEAVEN. I KNOW IT'S HARD FOR YOU TO UNDERSTAND RIGHT NOW."

DEAN SAYS, "OH YEAH, I UNDERSTAND. WE CAN COME BACK WHEN IT'S NOT THEIR BIRTHDAY, AND I CAN WRITE MY NAME ON THE TOMBSTONE. GRANDMA, I'M READY TO GO NOW."

DEAN SCREAMS, "HEY GRANDMA! WHY DO I HAVE TO WEAR A SEATBELT?"

GRANDMA SAYS, "DEAN, PLEASE STOP SCREAMING. USE YOUR INSIDE VOICE."

DEAN WHISPERS, "GRANDMA, ANSWER ME." GRANDMA ANSWERS, "DEAN, THERE ARE SEVERAL REASONS WHY YOU NEED TO WEAR A SEATBELT. WEARING A SEATBELT CAN SAVE YOUR LIFE. IT CAN ALSO PREVENT YOUR LITTLE BODY AND YOUR BONES FROM INJURIES. NOW, PUT THAT SEATBELT BACK ON!"

DEAN SAYS, "HEY GRANDMA! WHAT WILL I BE WHEN I GROW UP?"

GRANDMA REPLIES, "I LOVE THAT QUESTION! FIRST, LET ME ASK YOU, WHAT KIND OF THINGS DO YOU LIKE TO DO?"

DEAN SAYS, "I LIKE DOGS AND I LIKE TO PLAY MY VIDEO GAMES. I LIKE PLAYING FOOTBALL AND RUNNING ON THE TRACK!

GRANDMA SMILES AND SAYS, "YOU CAN BE AN ENGINEER, VETERINARIAN, PROFESSIONAL FOOTBALL PLAYER AND EVEN A TRACK STAR. THE SKY IS THE LIMIT! YOU CAN BE ANYTHING YOU WANT TO BE."

DEAN ASK, "CAN WE JUST GET ON THE HIGHWAY AND GO TO HEAVEN?"

GRANDMA LAUGHS AND SAYS, "WE CAN'T DRIVE TO HEAVEN. BUT, ONE DAY, GOD WILL DECIDE THE DAY WHEN WE WILL GO TO HEAVEN."

DEAN YELLS AND POINTS, "HEY GRANDMA! WHAT HAPPEN TO THAT MAN'S LEG? DID SOMEBODY TAKE IT?"

GRANDMA WHISPERS IN DEAN'S EAR, "DEAN, IT'S NOT NICE TO POINT AT PEOPLE."

DEAN SAYS, "BUT WHO TOOK HIS LEG?"

GRANDMA EXPLAINS, "THAT MAN IS IN A WHEELCHAIR BECAUSE HE CAN'T WALK. HE COULD HAVE POSSIBLY HAD AN ACCIDENT, OR HAVE BEEN SICK WITH A DISEASE AND HAD TO HAVE HIS LEG AMPUTATED. IT'S SO MANY REASONS WHY SOME PEOPLE MAY HAVE ONLY ONE LEG OR NO LEGS AT ALL."

DEAN ANGRILY SCREAMS OUT, "HEY GRANDMA! WHY DON'T I HAVE A DADDY? ALL MY FRIENDS HAVE ONE. THAT'S NOT FAIR!"

GRANDMA HUGS DEAN AND SAYS, "YOU HAVE A DADDY, UNFORTUNATELY YOUR FATHER HAS MADE UNWISE CHOICES AND DECIDED AT THIS TIME NOT TO BE APART OF YOUR LIFE, AND FOR THAT I AM SORRY. HE HAS NO IDEA OF THE GREATNESS YOU POSSESS. YOU ARE SO SPECIAL!"

DEAN ASK, "SO I'M SPECIAL?"

GRANDMA SAYS, "YOU ARE SUPER-DUPER SPECIAL! YOU DON'T EVER HAVE TO WORRY. THERE ARE TONS OF PEOPLE WHO ARE A PART OF YOUR LIFE, WHO LOVE YOU TO THE PIECES!"

GRANDMA LAUGHS, AND SAYS, "YES, YOUR FACE AND YOUR SKIN IS PERFECT. IT'S A BEAUTIFUL BROWN TONE OF SKIN. MY FACE IS NOT WHITE, I'M JUST A LIGHTER SHADE OF BROWN. THERE ARE SO MANY SKIN TONES IN OUR RACE. JUST SO YOU'LL UNDERSTAND, I INHERITED HALF OF MY SKIN TONE FROM MY MOM AND THE OTHER HALF FROM MY DAD. IT'S IN THE GENES."

DEAN SINGS OUT LOUDLY, "HEY GRANDMA! WHY IS MY HAIR CURLY AND MY FRIEND'S HAIR IS STRAIGHT?"

GRANDMA RUBS THE TOP OF HIS HAIR, AND SAYS, "EVERYONE'S HAIR IS DIFFERENT. YOUR HAIR IS SOFT LIKE YOUR MOMMY'S HAIR. IT'S NATURAL. I ABSOLUTELY LOVE YOUR HAIR! YOUR FRIEND'S HAIR IS PROBABLY STRAIGHT LIKE SOMEONE IN HIS FAMILY. JUST REMEMBER, WE NEVER JUDGE PEOPLE BY THEIR HAIR!"

DEAN WHISPERS TO GRANDMA, "HEY GRANDMA, WHY DO PEOPLE HAVE TO DIE? WILL I DIE IF I DON'T BEHAVE? I DON'T WANT TO DIE.

"SHHH, NOW LET'S LISTEN TO THE PASTOR."

GRANDMA HUGS DEAN AND WHISPERS," GOD LOVES YOU! EVERYONE WHO IS BORN INTO THE WORLD HAS TO DIE ONE DAY. WE CAN'T POSSIBLY LIVE FOREVER, BECAUSE WE ARE HUMAN BEINGS. ONLY GOD DECIDES WHEN OUR HEARTS NO LONGER WILL BEAT. BUT, THE GREAT THING ABOUT IT IS, WE WILL SEE EACH OTHER AGAIN. I PROMISE YOU THAT!"

DEAN LOOKS AT GRANDMA AND SAYS, "GRANDMA, SHHH, IT'S NOT NICE TO TALK IN CHURCH WHILE THE PASTOR IS TALKING."

DEAN LAUGHS AND SAYS, "HEY GRANDMA, WHY DO I HAVE TO TAKE A SHOWER? I TOOK ONE LAST WEEK."

GRANDMA GIGGLES, AND SAYS, "BOY, YOU BETTER GRAB YOUR LOOFAH AND BODY WASH AND START SCRUBBING! YOU HAVE GONE THROUGHOUT THE DAY, TOUCHING THINGS, SITTING DIFFERENT PLACES AND PLAYING AT THE PLAYGROUND. YOUR BODY IS DIRTY! TAKING A SHOWER REMOVES ALL THOSE DEAD SKIN CELLS AND GERMS OFF YOUR BODY."

GRANDMA SAYS, "DEAN, YOU WERE BORN A BOY, AND WILL ONE DAY BECOME A MAN. A STRONG, INTELLIGENT AND KIND MAN. THE MAN THAT YOU SEE, HE'S GOING TO BE ALRIGHT.

JUST UNDERSTAND, EVERYONE HAS CHOICES RELATING TO THEIR BODY AND HOW THEY WANT TO LOOK.

ONE THING FOR SURE, I LOVE YOU JUST AS YOU ARE.

HEY GRANDMA," YELLS DEAN, "HOW TALL WILL I BE WHEN I BECOME A MAN?"

GRANDMA EXPLAINS, "THE THINGS THAT WILL DETERMINE YOUR HEIGHT ARE THE THINGS YOU MUST DO NOW AND CONTINUE TO DO AS YOU GET OLDER. YOU MUST GET PLENTY OF REST. YOU MUST EAT THE RIGHT FOODS, ESPECIALLY THE YUCKY ONES THAT YOU DON'T LIKE. YOU MUST ALSO EXERCISE YOUR BODY AND BE SURE YOU ARE TAKING GOOD CARE OF IT."

"HEY GRANDMA!" YELLS DEAN, "LOOK AT THIS PICTURE OF MY MOMMY. HER STOMACH IS SO BIG! WAS MY MOMMY THERE WHEN I WAS BORN? HOW DID I COME OUT?"

GRANDMA GIGGLES, " OH YES, SHE WAS HUGE! SHE WAS 9 MONTHS PREGNANT. AND YES, SHE WAS THERE WHEN YOU WERE BORN. SHE WAS LAYING ON THE BED WHEN THE DOCTOR SWOOPED YOU UP FROM THE INSIDE OF HER STOMACH. EVERYONE IN THE HOSPITAL ROOM HAD TO BE VERY CAREFUL SO YOU COULD MAKE YOUR DEBUT."

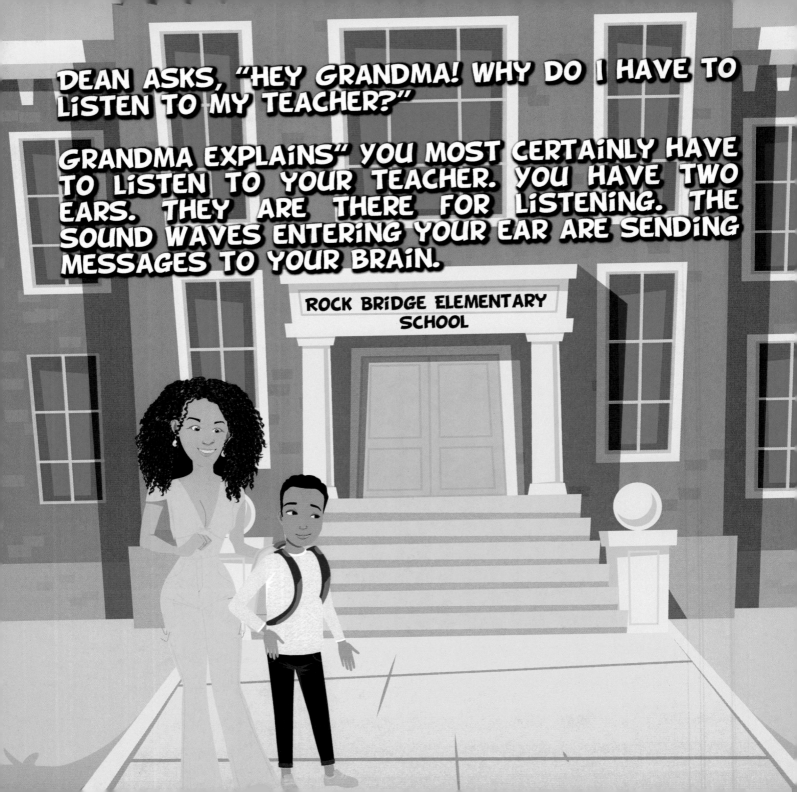

AS YOU SIT IN CLASS, IT IS IMPORTANT FOR YOU TO LISTEN TO YOUR TEACHER IN ORDER TO LEARN. AND FOLLOW DIRECTIONS. SHE IS ALSO TEACHING YOU NEW AND EXCITING THINGS AT SCHOOL.

DEAN SAYS, "BUT GRANDMA, MY TEACHER IS SO BORING! DUH!

"HEY GRANDMA!" DEAN INQUIRES, "I HAVE A QUESTION. I WAS WONDERING IF YOU LOVE ME?"

GRANDMA SMILES AND ANSWERS, " YES, INDEED!" I LOVED YOU BEFORE I MET YOU AND I'LL LOVE YOU ALWAYS."

DEAN CRIES OUT, "HEY GRANDMA! WHY DO I HAVE TO ALWAYS TAKE NAPS?"

GRANDMA SMILES AND SAYS, "HONESTLY, I'M THE ONE WHO NEEDS A NAP BECAUSE I'VE BEEN AROUND YOU ALL DAY. THIS GRANDMA IS TOTALLY WORN OUT! YOU HAVE BEEN VERY BUSY TODAY AND YOU NEED TO REST IN ORDER TO RE-REFUEL FOR LATER TODAY. YOUR BODY NEEDS A BREAK. THAT'S ALSO WHY YOU'RE A LITTLE GROUCHY RIGHT NOW."

"HEY GRANDMA!" YELLS DEAN. GRANDMA TURNS AROUND AND SAYS, "I'M RIGHT NEXT TO YOU, WHY ARE YOU ALWAYS SO LOUD?"

DEAN WHISPERS, "GRANDMA, WHY DO I HAVE TO WEAR UNDERWEAR?"

GRANDMA SAYS, "OH MY ! DEAN, UNDERWEAR IS A PART OF OUR EVERYDAY CLOTHING. IT KEEPS EVERYTHING IN PLACE WHILE YOU ARE WALKING, PLAYING AND EVEN SITTING DOWN. IT ALSO MAKES THE CLOTHES YOU WEAR MORE COMFORTABLE."

DEAN ASKS, "GRANDMA, DO YOU WEAR UNDERWEAR?"

GRANDMA LAUGHS AND SAYS,
"YES, I DO   EVERY SINGLE DAY.
GRANDMA SAYS, " NOW, HURRY UP AND GET
DRESSED".

DEAN SCREAMS OUT, "HEY GRANDMA! LOOK AT THAT MAN. HE IS NASTY. WHY IS HE SPITTING ON THE GROUND?"

GRANDMA LOOKS BEHIND HER AND SEES THE MAN. GRANDMA SAYS,

"AS PEOPLE ARE WALKING, THEY SOMETIMES HAVE THINGS IN THEIR THROAT THAT NEED TO COME OUT.

SO, AS THEY ARE WALKING, THEY JUST DECIDE TO SPIT ON THE SIDEWALK OR STREET."

DEAN LAUGHS LOUDLY AND YELLS, "HEY GRANDMA! WHY DO MY FEET STINK? COME AND SMELL MY FEET!"

GRANDMA HOLDS HER NOSE, AND THEN SAYS, "I'M NOT SMELLING YOUR STINKY FEET. I CAN SMELL THEM FROM ACROSS THE ROOM. UGH! THAT ODOR THAT YOU SMELL COMES FROM MOISTURE WITHIN YOUR SHOE. WHEN YOU WEAR SOCKS, IT PREVENTS YOUR FEET FROM SWEATING.

DEAN YELLS, "HEY GRANDMA! I FARTED, I FARTED! I FARTED!"

GRANDMA SAYS, "DEAN, THE ENTIRE NEIGHBORHOOD DIDN'T NEED TO KNOW THAT. IT'S A NATURAL THING PEOPLE DO."

DEAN ASK, "BUT WHY?"

GRANDMA EXPLAINS, "YOUR BODY HAS TO GET RID OF ALL THE FOODS, LIQUIDS AND OTHER THINGS IN YOUR STOMACH. IN THE PROCESS, YOU SWALLOW SMALL AMOUNTS OF AIR WHICH IS IN YOUR STOMACH. ALSO CALLED YOUR DIGESTIVE SYSTEM SOMETIMES WHEN YOU PASS GAS, YOU'VE EATEN SOMETHING THAT WAS DIFFICULT FOR YOUR LITTLE BODY TO DIGEST."

DEAN'S TOP SMARTY PANTS VOCABULARY FOR 5 YEARS OLD.

1. TOMBSTONE
2. INJURIES
3. LIMIT
4. DISTANCE
5. AMPUTATED
6. POSSESS
7. INHERITED
8. GENES
9. JUDGE
10. PROMISE
11. LOOFAH
12. CHOICES
13. GROWTH SPURT
14. SWOOPED
15. DEBUT
16. INQUIRE
17. RE-FUEL
18. SALIVA
19. DIGESTION- DIGESTIVE SYSTEM
20. MOISTURE

ABOUT THE AUTHOR

SCOTTIE B. CALDWELL, A GRADUATE OF LANE COLLEGE IN JACKSON, TN. SHE ALSO RECEIVED HER MASTERS IN ADMINISTRATION AND SUPERVISION FROM TREVECCA NAZARENE AND EARNED HER EDUCATIONAL SPECIALIST DEGREE IN CURRICULUM AND INSTRUCTION DEGREE FROM TENNESSEE TECHNOLOGICAL UNIVERSITY.

SHE RETIRED IN 2015 FROM HAMILTON COUNTY SCHOOLS IN CHATTANOOGA, TN.

SHE IS PASSIONATE ABOUT THE ARTS. SHE ENJOYS PHOTOGRAPHY, ACTING IN FILMS AND SCREEN PLAYS. HER LOVE FOR WRITING HAS LEAD HER TO DIRECTING AND PRODUCING FROM HER VERY OWN MEDIA.DIVA. PRODUCTIONS.

ABOUT THE AUTHOR

DEAN CHRISTOPHER CALDWELL IS 6 YEARS OLD. HE IS A FIRST GRADE STUDENT AT ROCKBRIDGE ELEMENTARY SCHOOL IN ATLANTA, GA. DEAN'S HOBBIES INCLUDE FOOTBALL, TRACK, BASKETBALL AND PLAYING VIDEO GAMES. HE ENJOYS MATHEMATICAL CHALLENGES AND PLAYING CHESS. HE ALSO ADORES SPENDING TIME WITH HIS GRANDPA ALAN HIS SUPER HERO IS HIS MOM, CHRISTIAN CALDWELL.

HEY GRANDMA!

This book is about the relationship between a grandma and her grandson. Dean is a 5 year old with a burning curiosity about life's essential questions. His grandma may not have all the correct answers, but she addresses his questions so he can understand to the best of his ability.

WRITTEN BY:

SCOTTIE B. CALDWELL AND DEAN CHRISTOPHER CALDWELL

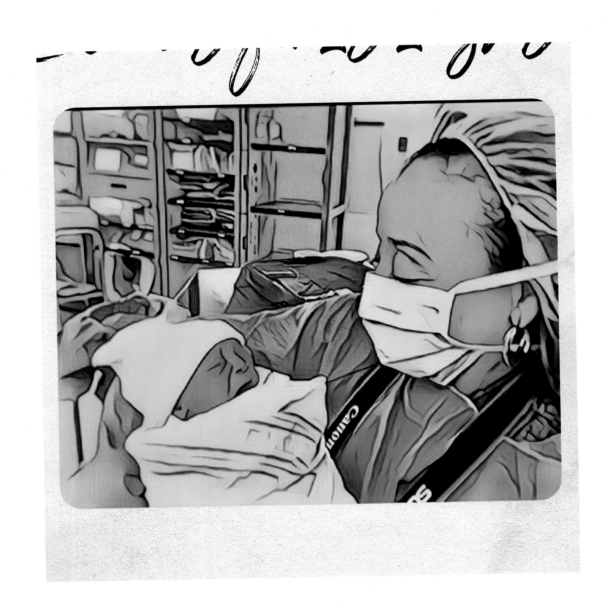

Made in United States
Orlando, FL
28 July 2023